Aesop's Fables

Retold by
CAROL WATSON

Illustrated by
NICK PRICE

CONTENTS

Series Editor: Heather Amery

Reading Expert: Betty Root
Centre for the Teaching of Reading
University of Reading

The Tortoise and the Hare

One day a silly hare sat talking to his friends. He was boasting as usual.

"I can run faster than any of you," he said. "No one can possibly beat me in a race."

He turned to the old tortoise. "You walk so slowly, I don't know why you bother at all."

"I may be slow," said the tortoise, "but I bet I can get to the end of this field before you."

"The tortoise wants a race!" laughed the hare. His friends gathered round to watch.

"I'll win easily," giggled the hare as he and the tortoise lined up ready to start.

2

"Ready, steady go!" shouted the badger. Everyone cheered as the hare raced away.

The tortoise moved off slowly. She plodded quietly along towards the end of the field.

The hare stopped halfway. "That old tortoise will take all day," he thought. "I'll have a little rest."

Soon he fell fast asleep and he did not wake up for hours.

He spotted the tortoise near the finish and ran as fast as he could. But it was too late. "I told you I'd get there before you," said the tortoise.

Those who are slow and sure often win in the end.

The Crow and the Jug

One hot day a thirsty crow was searching for something to drink. He pecked at the earth.

The ground was hard and all the streams had dried up. There was no water anywhere.

In the distance he saw a jug on a cottage windowsill. He flew over to have a look.

"Ah, there's water at the bottom," he cawed, peering down. But he could not reach it.

The crow felt more and more thirsty. He pecked hard at the jug but it would not break.

"I'll push it over," he said to himself, but the jug was so heavy it would not move.

Then he had an idea.
He flew off to a pile
of pebbles and picked
one up in his beak.

The crow flew back,
dropped the pebble into
the jug and then went
off to find another.

The crow dropped so
many pebbles into the
jug they pushed the
water up to the top.

At last he had a long,
cool drink. "All my
hard work was worth it
in the end," he thought.

If you try hard enough you will get what you want.

The Ant and the Dove

 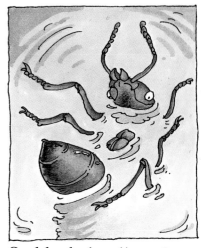

As an ant was crawling home to his nest one day, he went past a sparkling fountain.

"What a beautiful sight," he thought. He went nearer to have a better look.

Suddenly he slipped. He slithered over the edge and fell into the water.

Just at that moment a dove was flying over the fountain. She saw the tiny ant drowning.

She quickly flew to a tree nearby and picked a leaf from it with her beak.

"Here you are," she called. She dropped the leaf close to the struggling ant.

Gasping for breath, he climbed on to the leaf. Then he floated safely to dry land.

Next day the ant saw the dove looking for worms. A man was creeping up behind her.

He wanted to catch the bird and take her home. "Got you," he cried and he trapped the gentle dove in his net.

The ant ran over to the man. He crawled up his leg and bit him hard.

"Ouch!" yelled the man, jumping up and down. He dropped the net and clutched his leg.

The dove hopped out of the net and flew away to safety. "Thank you," she cooed to the ant.

One good turn deserves another.

The Dog in the Manger

The dog trotted into the stable. He sniffed around for food, but he could not find anything at all to eat.

One day a hungry dog was looking for food. He passed by a stable. A horse was peering out. "Hello," he said.

"Have you got anything to eat?" asked the dog. "Plenty!" said the friendly horse, "Come in and have some."

"There's nothing in here but hay," he growled. "But that's what we eat," said one of the cows.

8

"I can't eat that," said the dog angrily. He climbed into a manger full of hay and went to sleep.

When the animals came to eat the hay the dog snarled at them and would not let them near. "We want our dinner," said the cow.

"It's no good to you," added the horse. "If I can't eat it," said the selfish dog, "I'm not going to let you have it either."

Don't stop others having what you don't want.

The Town Mouse and the Country Mouse

Once there was a little brown mouse. He lived in a nest under a hedge in the countryside.

He was happy living there. His nest was cosy and warm and he had plenty to eat.

One day his cousin from town came to stay. He wanted to see what country life was like.

The country mouse made him comfortable and gave him his best bed to sleep on.

Next morning, when they had breakfast, the town mouse said rudely "This food is horrible."

"It's so dull here," he went on. "Life in town is much more fun. Come and stay with me."

So off they went. On the way the town mouse told stories about all the food they would eat.

"Here we are at last," he said, pointing to a large house. They crept in under the back door.

The town mouse led the way into a grand dining room. The table was covered with food left over from dinner.

The country mouse was thrilled. "I've never seen such a feast," he squeaked. They started to gobble up the food.

"Keep very still," whispered the town mouse. The man picked up an apple, then he went out of the room.

Suddenly the door opened and light filled the room. The mice ran to hide behind the cheese.

They saw a man come into the room. He walked over to the table and peered into the fruit bowl.

The town mouse began to eat again, but the country mouse was so frightened he could not eat any more.

In the corner of the room there was a large, fat cat. The mice had woken him up.

He heard a munching sound coming from the table and he padded across the room.

"A cat!" cried the country mouse. The cat sprang on to the table and swiped at the mouse with his claws.

"Follow me!" cried his cousin and they ran into a mouse hole.

The country mouse had never been so scared in all his life. He did not like the town at all.

"Goodbye, cousin," he said. "I'm going back to the country where life is quiet but safe."

It is better to live a simple, quiet life than a rich, dangerous one.

The Fox and the Crow

It was a fox. He saw the cheese and wanted it for himself. He smiled at the crow.

Once an old crow stole a lump of cheese. She carried it away to the nearest tree.

Just as she was about to eat the cheese, she heard a noise on the ground below her.

"Oh lovely crow!" he said. "Your eyes are so bright and your feathers are so lovely."

The crow was very pleased and ruffled up her feathers. She believed the fox.

The crow opened her beak to give a loud 'caw' and the cheese fell to the ground.

"You are such a beautiful bird," he went on, "I'm sure you must sing sweetly too."

The fox quickly gobbled it up. He looked up at the crow with a wicked smile on his face.

"Thank you," he said. "You may have a voice, but you certainly have no brains!"

Don't always believe people who flatter you.

15

The Lion and the Mouse

One hot day a big lion lay sleeping in the sun. A tiny mouse ran along the ground carrying some corn. She was in such a hurry she did not notice the lion.

By mistake she ran over his paw. Her feet and whiskers tickled the lion and woke him up.

"What's this?" he snarled, grabbing the mouse in his claws. He licked his lips hungrily.

"Please don't eat me," the mouse squeaked. "If you let me go I will help you one day."

The lion laughed loudly "How can a tiny mouse like you help me?" he said, but he let her go.

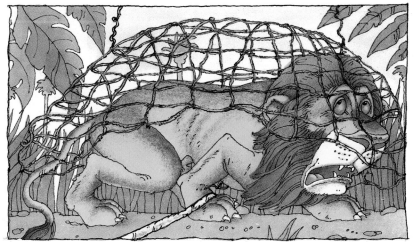

The next day the lion went out hunting. As he ran he tripped on a rope across the path.

Suddenly a large net fell on him. He was caught in a trap and could not get out.

He struggled and pulled, and he growled and roared. His cries were heard all over the jungle.

Far away the mouse heard the lion's roar. She ran to find him.

The mouse gnawed and nibbled at the net until at last the lion was free.

"Thank you, little mouse," said the huge lion. "You did help me after all."

Little friends are often great friends.

17

The Dog and the Bone

One day a hungry dog crept into a butcher's shop and stole a large, juicy bone.

He wanted to eat the bone in peace, so he ran away with it into the countryside.

Soon he came to a stream. It had a little bridge over it and he began to cross.

Suddenly he stopped. He saw another dog staring up at him from the water.

The other dog had a bone in his mouth too. "That bone is bigger than mine," he thought. He growled. The dog seemed to growl back.

18

He wanted the other bone so much, he barked angrily at the other dog.

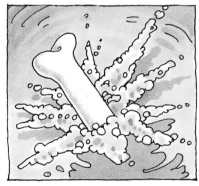

As he opened his mouth to bark the bone fell out. It dropped into the water and sank.

When the water grew calm again the dog saw that he was staring at himself in the stream. There was no other dog.

"Now I don't have a bone at all," he thought sadly. "I wish I hadn't been so greedy."

Be content with what you have.

The Grasshopper and the Ant

"I'm collecting corn for the winter," said the ant. "You should do the same yourself."

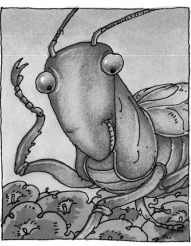

One summer's day a grasshopper was dancing in the sun. He saw a tiny ant hurrying by.

She looked very tired and hot. "Why are you working on such a lovely day?" asked the grasshopper.

"I'm enjoying the summer," laughed the grasshopper. "I can't think about winter.

The ant went on her way. She joined all the other ants carrying food to their store.

When winter came and snow was on the ground, the grasshopper had nothing to eat.

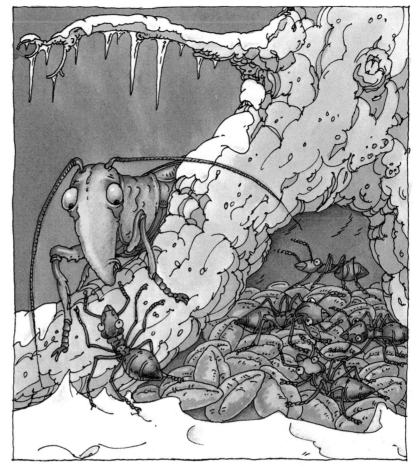

He was so hungry he begged the ants to give him food. "We worked all summer to collect our corn. What were you doing then?" said one of the ants.

"I was busy dancing," cried the grasshopper. "If you can dance all summer and do no work," one ant said crossly, "then you must starve in the winter."

Always try to save for a rainy day.

The Fox and the Stork

One evening a fox invited a stork to dinner. When the stork arrived she was very hungry. She was looking forward to a tasty meal. "Welcome!" said the fox.

He went to the kitchen and brought out two dishes of hot soup. It smelt delicious.

The fox gave one dish of soup to the stork and then he greedily lapped up his own.

Try as she might, the stork could not drink the soup. Her beak was too long and narrow for the shallow dish.

"Don't you like it," grinned the cunning fox. "Let me help you." And he lapped up the stork's dinner as well.

The stork went home hungry. She knew the fox had tricked her and she was very angry.

The next week the stork invited the fox to dinner. "Come in," she said "Dinner's ready."

The stork put the soup in two tall, thin jars. She gave one to the fox and then began to eat from her own.

The fox could not reach his soup. His nose was too short for the tall, thin jar. He licked the edge hungrily.

23

"Let me help you," said the clever stork and she quickly ate up the fox's dinner.

This time the fox went home hungry. "I've been caught out by my own trick," he sighed.

If you play mean tricks on people, they may play them on you.

First published in 1982 by Usborne Publishing Ltd. Usborne House, 83-85 Saffron Hill London EC1N 8RT, England

Printed in Hong Kong / China